Disney's
HOME
On The
RANGE

ADVANCE
PUBLISHERS

Published by Advance Publishers, L.C.
Maitland, FL 32751 USA
www.advancepublishers.com
Produced by Judy O Productions, Inc.
Designed by SunDried Penguin
© 2006 Disney Enterprises, Inc.
Home on the Range
Printed in the United States of America

Out in the Wild West there was a lovely little farm called Patch of Heaven. On Patch of Heaven all the animals were a part of the family. Pearl ran the farm with a little help from her three cows Mrs Caloway, Grace and her most recent addition, Maggie.

One day, the sheriff arrived on his horse, Buck, with some bad news. He handed Pearl a bank notice that said she had three days to settle her debt of $750, or they'd auction off Patch of Heaven. Maggie refused to give up, though, and set off into town with Grace and Mrs Caloway to find the sheriff's horse and ask him to give them more time.

In town, Buck was dreaming of capturing outlaws with Rico the famous bounty hunter when the cows found him. Just then, Rico rode into town and tossed yet another outlaw on to the sheriff's porch. "The only varmint left is that low-down, good for nothin' Alameda Slim," said the sheriff. Slim was a cattle thief, who with the help of the Willie Brothers, would steal an entire herd of cows, and they'd just disappear. The bounty on Slim was $750! Maggie had an idea – if the cows captured Slim they could save the farm!

"Look, all we gotta do is follow the chuck wagon to a cattle drive and then, you see, the bad guys come to us!" Maggie told the others, and they set off. But that night Slim turned up on his buffalo, Junior, and began to yodel – it was his secret cow-rustling weapon. Maggie, Mrs Caloway and the cattle fell into a trance and followed Slim – but the music didn't affect Grace. Instead she pushed the wagon downhill after the other cows – where it scooped them up away from the herd.

Down in the canyon, Rico
turned up riding … Buck!
They started chasing Slim,
but in a flash, he and the
Willies disappeared with
the stolen herd!

Meanwhile Slim, the Willies and the stolen herd were hiding in an abandoned mine. Slim had changed into a clever disguise he wore to buy land unnoticed. It was all part of his plan – steal the cattle, force the ranchers to go broke and sell their land. Then, in disguise, he'd buy it cheap. Now, Slim was greedily looking at his map, pointing out … Patch of Heaven!

The next day, the cows met a jack rabbit named Lucky Jack, who told them his mine had been taken over by an outlaw. The cows realized it was Slim, so Lucky Jack and the cows made their way towards the mine's entrance. Buck was already there, but he couldn't get inside. "The only critters that get by me are cows!" said Junior, who was blocking the entrance. Buck stared in disbelief as the three cows walked right past Junior, carrying Lucky Jack.

Now all they had to do was capture Slim. "You two get his attention while I sneak up behind him," Maggie instructed the cows. "Then I'll knock him into the cart. And then we'll rope him up and wheel him to justice!" Slim spotted the cows and began to yodel, but Maggie and Mrs Caloway had plugged their ears. Before Slim knew what was happening, the cows pushed him into a mine cart while Lucky Jack conked him on the head.

But the mine cart rolled away from the cows and out of control ... with Slim still in it. The cows raced after them in another mine cart, with everyone chasing after them. Then they all landed on the tracks outside the mine with a big crash!

Slim burst out of his cart, grabbed the cows and handed them over to the Willies, before he threw a bundle of money to Rico – yep, Rico was really Slim's partner! Then he rode off disguised as land baron Yancy O'Del, to buy Patch of Heaven at the bank auction. But Buck and the girls weren't about to give up. They helped each other capture and tie up Rico and the Willies.

Then the cows jumped on to the train and drove it straight to Patch of Heaven. They arrived just in time. The three cows charged at Slim – with the help of all the farm animals. "It's Alameda Slim!" cried the sheriff and he threw a lasso around the outlaw, before taking him away.

The cows had fought the baddest outlaw in the West – and won. They'd also saved the farm. The next day the whole gang posed together for a picture in the local newspaper. The three cows were famous, and they were finally home!

The End